The Counting Race

For my parents, Frank and Mary—MM

ISBN 0-439-57461-7

Published by Scholastic Inc., 557 Broadway, New York, NY 10012, by arrangement with Aladdin Paperbacks, Simon & Schuster Children's Publishing Division. SCHOLASTIC and associated logos are trademarks and/or registered trademarks of Scholastic Inc.

12 11 10 9 8 9/0

Printed in the U.S.A. 23

First Scholastic printing, October 2003

Book design by Sammy Yuen Jr.
The text for this book was set in CentSchbook BT.

The Counting Race

Written by Margaret McNamara
Illustrated by Mike Gordon

SCHOLASTIC INC.
New York Toronto London Auckland Sydney
Mexico City New Delhi Hong Kong Buenos Aires

“We are having
a race today,”
said Mrs. Connor.

The first graders
loved races.

"A running race?"
asked Reza.

"An eating race?"
asked Katie.

“No,” said Mrs. Connor,
“a counting race.”
“What is a counting race?”
asked Hannah.

"I am going to see
if you can count to ten
in one second,"
said Mrs. Connor.

"That is so easy,"
said James.

"I'll go first,"
said Michael.
"One, two, three, four,
five, six—"

“Out of time,”
said Mrs. Connor.

"My turn," said Neil.
"One, two, three, four,
five, six, seven—"

"Sorry, Neil,"
said Mrs. Connor.

"Me next!" said Eigen.
"One, two, three, four,
five, six, seven, eight—"
"Close!" said Mrs. Connor.

Hannah put up her hand.
"Mrs. Connor, can all
the first graders
work on this
together?" she asked.

“Yes, Hannah,”
said Mrs. Connor.

All the first graders
got together.

They talked loudly.

They talked quietly.

They had an idea.

“Ask us to race again,
Mrs. Connor,”
said Megan.

"Okay," said Mrs. Connor.
"Can you count to ten
in one second?"

All together,
the first graders said,

"Two! Four!
Six! Eight!
Ten!"

"You did it,"
said Mrs. Connor.
"Good for you!"

"We counted by twos,"
said Emma.
"It is a faster way
to count," said James.

"Here is one more question," said Mrs. Connor.

"Two, four, six, eight.
Who do I appreciate?"
The children knew
the answer.

"Us!" they said.

And they were right again.